I Will Not I

T0208190

Madinah Nakandha Kisubi

FOUNTAIN PUBLISHERS
Kampala

Fountain Publishers Ltd
P. O. Box 488 Kampala
E-mail:fountain@starcom.co.ug
Website:www.fountain@starcome.co.ug

Distributed in Europe, North America and Australia by
African Books Collective (ABC),
P.O. Box 721, Oxford OX1 9EN, UK.
Tel:+44(0) 1869 349110 Fax: +44(0)1869 349110
Email: orders@africanbookscollective.com
Website: www.africanbookscollective.com

ISBN 978-9970-02-761-3

Author's Note

This book is about the trials and tribulations, the challenges, hopes and opportunities that confront the girl-child as she grows up. In many parts of Africa, children are born in societies and communities where their destiny seems to be already determined upon birth. Boys are expected to grow up and become the breadwinners and they are brought up to fill that role. They are given priority in education, have a right to land and property, and have dominance over the girls. They are the natural heirs to the parents and they are taken as the guarantors of continuation of their respective lineages. Unfortunately, the girls are socialised to stay at home, to become wives and homemakers. They till the soil and ensure food sufficiency. They are forced to drop out of school at an early age in order to be married off, frequently to obtain bride wealth for their brothers. They are relegated to the kitchen and the home. Their world is limited to the house and housework.

This story is about a girl – Namukose – that has, in spite of all the trials and tribulations, community and tribal demarcations and constraints, in spite of unquestioned cultural norms, succeeded in achieving her dreams. Namukose makes it to school; she gets inspired by the day; becomes more confident with every challenge and success; and gets determined and hopeful that one day, she will become the breadwinner and the homemaker. She believes that one day she will be able to ensure a better life for her parents and children, be able to break through all barriers and challenges on the road to women's emancipation, their development, contribution to the well-being of society, and empowerment.

Namukose's story is an inspiration to all girl-children from all walks of life, from every community, and from every society where a girl has the same challenges in life and should be given the same opportunities if we are to make this world a better place to live, a world in which everyone will be happy and useful.

The story takes place in a rural village in Uganda that is devoid of the pleasures that modernity and development bring, a rural village deprived of most of what is taken for granted in modern life – sources of clean water, electricity, good roads. Yet in spite of all this, Namukose succeeds.

Madinah Nakandha Kisubi

Chapter One

Chairman Edwin Bukenya was a strong man. A proud man. A man who knew the value of hard work. He had raised himself from very humble beginnings to the position of Local Council Chairman of this village through the sweat of his back and through the determination to succeed. It had not been an easy journey, and he knew why – if he had managed to get an education, it would have not been as hard. But in the days of his youth, many families, like his, were poor. Many children, like him, had to drop out of school because their parents just could not afford to pay the fees.

That is why he felt that this meeting he had called was very important. He stood up and coughed, before addressing the men and women of the village, who had gathered under in the church yard.

"Welcome to this meeting," he began.

The villagers had been chatting among themselves, but the moment their chairman spoke, they all fell silent and looked up to listen.

"I have called you to talk about Universal Primary Education. As you might have heard over the radio, the government has started a programme in which all children of school-going age are supposed to go to school. It caters for four children from each family. It is through education that we will be able to fight poverty. As representatives of the government, we have been requested to ensure that the programme succeeds. We have to make sure that both girls and boys are in school."

After the chairman finished speaking, a slow mumble began to rise from the villagers, as they took in what he had said, and collected their thoughts. Basule was the first one to speak out loud. He said, "I think it is fine that we can now have some of our children educated for free. My worry is, however, about the girls whom we have been

1

told to send to school. The way I see it, educating a girl is like watering your friend's garden!"

"What do you mean?" asked the chairman.

"You don't gain anything by educating a girl. The only people who gain are the family she will get married into," Basule explained.

"I do not agree," said the chairman. "The family she marries into is not the only one that benefits. Educating the girl-child enables her to look after herself, first of all, so your daughters will benefit also. Plus, she is able to take better care of her family, so you also benefit. We need to respond to the government's call to educate the girl-child."

Bugyabukye in the corner at the back was shaking his head vigorously. He was not pleased by any of this. He raised his hand, but did not wait to be called upon to speak before he started talking. "You want us to educate girls? Don't you know that a girl's place is in the kitchen? Why waste time and money on a girl? In any case, many educated women end up in the kitchen cooking, cleaning the house and looking after the children. They do the same work that my wife does, and yet she has never seen a blackboard!"

"He is right, Chairman," said Nabutono. "Girls will spend a lot of time in school. When will they ever learn how to cook and care for children? Who will marry such girls who cannot prepare good meals for their husbands?"

The chairman had known that the villagers would not welcome the idea of educating their girls, but he had not expected this much resistance. Even Nabutono, a woman herself, was against it?

"You can teach them all that on the weekends. They don't have school on weekends," he said, firmly.

"Is that enough time?" asked Musubika. But before he could answer, Basule was speaking again. "Most men do not want to marry educated women by the way. They become wiseacres and they think that because they have been to school they don't need to obey their husbands. Men want women who will not argue with them all the time."

"So if they can't get married we don't even get bride price from them?" asked Musubika again, liking the idea less and less as the discussion proceeded. "You take your daughters to school and you will die poor men."

The chairman was becoming annoyed. "Are your daughters just something to sell? Like cattle and goats? Don't you want to help them have better lives?" he scolded.

"The more girls you have the richer you become," Kidhozi said. "That is the advantage of having girls instead of boys."

"As for me, I am a farmer. I need my children on the farm seven days a week. Who will scare the birds away from the rice fields if I let the children go to school? That is children's work and they enjoy doing it. At my age I cannot be out in the field shouting like a mental case," said Bugyabukye finally.

"Have you ever heard of scarecrows?" asked the chairman impatiently.

"You cannot compare scarecrows to children. Children are more effective in chasing away the birds." Bugyabukye stomped his stick on the ground to show that he was not going to change his mind.

The chairman paused. He could see that he was losing his temper, and that would not help anyone. He took a deep breath. "But you are talking as if you cannot see for yourselves that educated children help. Look at Magezi. He educated all his children and now they look after him in his old age. Your children will help you if you send them to school. That is why you should all send your children to school on Monday."

"But they are our children..." Nabutono began to argue, but the chairman stopped her in the middle of her speech.

"I know they are your children. But on Monday, you are sending them to school. That is the new rule!"

The villagers argued more, but the chairman remained adamant. He knew that it was for the good of the children; so that they would have better chances in life than he himself had had.

The Mukose family lived at the far end of the village, where the grass-thatched houses were built, away from the tin-roofed houses in the centre.

They had a small house with two rooms – a bedroom and a sitting room.

It was a small family. Mukose and his wife Jane had two children: Seven-year-old Namukose and a five-year-old boy, Bogere. When Namukose was born, Jane had been excited to see her newborn, but Mukose didn't feel as proud. He had wanted a boy – a potential successor.

Even the friends and family members who came in to visit the new parents and welcome the baby said that they hoped that Mukose and his wife would soon be blessed with a baby boy.

Two years later, Bogere came along. Now the four of them lived together in the tiny house. Namukose and her brother slept in the sitting room, on a mat, and covered themselves with a piece of cloth that had once belonged to their mother.

Namukose had never gone to school. Her family was too poor.

This made her mother unhappy because she wanted her children to go to school and have a better life than hers. She never had the chance to get an education. Her own parents having felt that only the boys should go to school, Jane and her sisters stayed at home and did housework and farm chores.

When she was fifteen years old, Jane was married off to Mukose and life continued to be all about hard work. She worked their small plot single-handedly every day, while her husband spent all his time in the trading centre away from the village. He only came home to eat and sleep.

"Will you let Namukose go to school?" she asked him one evening when he returned from the trading centre and was preparing to eat his supper.

He shrugged. He didn't seem to think it was any of his business what happened to them. "Since it is free, why not?" he said, focusing his attention on the food.

Jane did not show it, but her heart was full of joy.

When Namukose returned from the well, her mother met her outside the home and broke the good news to her.

"You will go to school tomorrow," she said.

Namukose could not believe her ears. This was like a dream come true for her.

She remembered the time Namaganda, the girl from the next house, had tried to teach her how to write her name. It was difficult. Namukose had failed to do it.

"You are old enough to go to school. Teachers can help you better," Namaganda had said.

When Namukose went home that day, she had begged her mother to take her to school. But her mother had told her that there was no money to pay her school fees. She wept but that did not help. So she stayed at home, doing housework and looking after her younger brother, Bogere.

But now she was finally getting the chance to go to school! She was overjoyed. She sat down next to her mother.

"Which dress am I going to wear, Mama?" she asked.

"The one you use for going to church," said her mother.

She dashed into the house to check on the dress. It had been laid out and folded, ready for her to wear to church on Sunday.

Namukose had a lot on her mind as she went to bed at night. She was not sure who she was going to meet at school. The only person she knew was Namaganda. She was not sure how she would be received at school. She was not sure about they would expect of her and, most important of all, whether she would be able to wake up in time to go to school. She kept on pinching herself to keep awake. But she still fell asleep.

Chapter Two

The next day – the day Namukose was to start school – was beautiful and sunny.

Namukose was wearing her smart Sunday dress, and was very clean. She had washed her face, brushed her teeth and combed her hair. Her mother had also put on a nice dress. They walked together hand in hand. It was a long journey – one kilometre – and they were both barefoot, but they were also both happy.

When they arrived at the school Namukose felt a bit exhausted, though she was excited and nervous at the same time. There were so many children at the school, and they all seemed busy. Some were playing in the compound, others were sweeping the classrooms. Namukose wondered where she would fit in. One of the pupils saw them and walked up to them. The pupil, a tall girl with a tie on her school uniform, introduced herself as a prefect (Namukose wondered what the word "prefect" meant) and greeted Mrs Mukose.

Mrs Mukose asked for directions to the headteacher's office.

The prefect was helpful and led the two of them to a building near the edge of the compound. Mrs Mukose knocked on the door, as Namukose watched the prefect return to the other pupils; thinking how smart she looked, and how confident! How Namukose wanted to be like her.

"Come in," said Mr Bateganya, the headmaster, when he heard a knock on the door. "You are welcome. Have a seat."

They entered a room that was small, but tidy. The floor was freshly swept and, the windows open, letting in the bright morning sunlight. The walls were covered with charts in different colours – blue, pink and yellow. The charts showed the different parts of the human body, different animals and plants, the President and his ministers and some of them were maps of Africa and of Uganda. In the middle of the room, underneath the window, there was a table and a chair on which Mr Bateganya was seated.

Mr Bateganya had a bald head, and was smartly dressed in a blue long-sleeved shirt and black trousers with black shoes.

"Good morning Sir," greeted Mrs Mukose.

"Good morning," replied the headmaster. "Can I help you?"

"I am Mrs Jane Mukose," she answered. "I would like my daughter to start school."

The headmaster rose and leaned over to Namukose. He smiled kindly at her and asked, "Young lady, you would like to join our school? That is good news. We need more young ladies in school. What is your name?"

"My name is Lucy Namukose," replied Namukose, shyly.

"Welcome, Lucy," said the kind man, shaking her hand before he stood up straight and shook her mother's hand as well. "Have a seat, Mrs Mukose. Your application was finalized successfully and, even though you joined us late, we were able to finish your registration on time. We made a place for your daughter in Primary One. We welcome you both to Buwabe Primary School", said the headmaster. He wrote her name down. Then he wrote down her mother's name and called out to the prefect who had brought them and instructed her to lead Namukose to the Primary One class.

Namukose looked at her mother with fear on her face.

"Everything will be fine," her mother reassured her. "Most of the pupils in your class are new like you."

As the other pupil led her away, she waved to her mother and went off to class leaving Mrs Mukose in the headmaster's office.

When they were gone, Mr Bateganya told Jane Mukose, "Under UPE you are supposed to provide your child with pens, pencils, books and uniform, and you are supposed to feed the child at school. The government takes care of the school dues."

Namukose's mother listened attentively. She was relieved that she would not have to ask her husband for money.

"Will you pick Namukose up at lunch time?" asked the headmaster.

"No, she has a friend in Primary Two called Namaganda. They will come back together," replied Namukose's mother.

The headmaster asked her more questions about Namukose and about her family. He wrote it all down in the UPE register. He told her about the school and what would be expected of her.

Meanwhile in class, the teacher recorded Namukose's name in the register. There were many pupils in the class. They were all standing to greet the teacher.

"Good morning class," greeted the teacher.

"Good morning teacher," the children responded.

"Sit down."

"Thank you, Miss Nandase."

Since Namukose was taller than most pupils, she was made to sit at the back of the class. She sat next to a girl who was almost her own size. The other girl was called Wotali. Unlike Namukose, Wotali was dressed in a uniform and brought along exercise books and a pencil. Namukose looked at the other girl and realised that she was more prepared than her.

The teacher, Miss Nandase, was an elderly woman who had been teaching for twenty-five years. She had become a teacher after lack of school fees forced her to drop out of secondary school. She resolved, then, to dedicate her life to helping other children succeed in their education.

She started, the day's lesson by writing the number one, on the chalkboard.

Then she looked into the class and Namusoke was shocked when her eyes alighted on her! "The new girl,

Namukose, should come up and write this number on the board next to the one I have written."

Namukose felt a lump rise in her throat. She felt her knees shake as she stood up. She could feel all the other pupils watching her as she walked to the blackboard.

But she took a deep breath and thought of her mother. That gave her courage. She picked up a piece of chalk and wrote the number one – neatly – on the blackboard next to the number Miss Nandase had written.

The teacher asked the whole class to clap for her, and they did. Hearing the whole class congratulating her felt good. She could feel a smile creeping across her face as she walked back to her desk. She forgot all her nervousness then and enjoyed the rest of the lesson. She was glad that she was learning how to count.

The rest of the day was exciting. There were lots of new things to learn and lots of fun. Some of them were a bit difficult to understand at first, but the teachers always helped all the children who had problems. They were kind and gentle. Namukose spent her first day of school smiling, and when the bell rang and it was time to go home, she was still smiling as she looked for Namaganda among the Primary Two girls, so that they could walk home together. As they walked, they talked all about school life. Namukose was full of questions, and Namaganda answered them all. She told her stories about teachers and class and the other pupils and they laughed all the way home. By the time they reached home, it was as if the distance was much shorter than it had been when Namukose and her mother set off that morning.

Namukose was very hungry when she reached her home. She ran straight to the kitchen where her mother was preparing lunch.

"Welcome back, Namukose," called her mother. "How was school?"

"It was fun!" Namukose answered, her voice full of excitement. She couldn't wait to tell her mother all about it. She launched into it right away. "Our teacher taught us how to count. She also said we should take counters to school tomorrow. Mummy, at school there are both men and women who are teachers! Our class teacher is called Miss Nandase. I did not know that women work away from home. She treats us very well. She is like a mother to us."

"What does she do?" asked Mrs Mukose.

"She tells children to clean their faces and blow their noses whenever they forget to do so."

"That is good."

"There are also rules that we have to follow. We have to keep time; we always have to be in the right place at the right time."

"How do you manage to remember all that?" Mrs Mukose asked.

"The teacher reminds us and the bell controls every activity at school. If it is time for break, the teacher tells us, 'You can go for break.'"

Suddenly Namukose asked her mother a question: "Mummy, do you know how to read and write?"

Her mother answered sadly, "No, dear, I don't."

"Why not?" Namukose asked again.

"When we were young it was rare for girls to be sent to school. Parents preferred to take boys to school. Girls remained at home to help with the housework. The parents said that a woman's place was in the kitchen."

Namukose felt sorry for her mother.

The following day Namukose was so eager to go to school that she rushed through her breakfast with great speed. Then she picked up her books, which she had put in a polythene bag, and ran out of the house to start the journey to school. Her class teacher had told them to keep time, and the school prefects, who were older pupils whose job was to help keep the rules, were always on the lookout for pupils who came late.

She had ran part of the way and walked fast as much as she could, and she just managed to get there on time.

11

As soon as she arrived at the school, the bell rang. All the pupils assembled and the prefects began the daily routine of checking for pupils who were untidy. They checked hair and nails and whether their clothes were clean. Any pupil who was not neat was made to stand in front of the whole school. This is what the pupils feared most.

After the checking, the whole school was led in prayer by the prefect on duty and then the pupils went off into their respective classes. In class, the teacher helped the pupils to write their names on their exercise books. Then the books were kept in the cupboard in a corner of the classroom.

In Primary One, a teacher has a lot to teach. She does not only teach what is on the syllabus. The teacher also has to teach things like personal hygiene to the children. That was why Miss Nandase had to teach the pupils how to use the latrine.

She drew a square shape on the floor and asked the pupils to come in front of the class. She asked one of the pupils, a boy called Kabugudhe, to demonstrate to others how he would use the latrine. Most of the pupils covered their faces. They felt shy. However, Kabugudhe was a courageous boy. He squatted in the middle of the square to demonstrate how to use the latrine and the teacher asked the rest of the class to clap for him. She then took them to the real latrine and taught them to always wash their hands after using it.

The next lesson was story time.

"Who can tell us a story?" asked the teacher.

Some pupils raised their hands. Namukose felt too shy to put up her hand.

"Namukose, can you tell us a story?" asked Miss Nandase, even though Namukose had not raised her hand.

Namukose's heart beat fast. Slowly she moved to the front of the class. She mumbled something. "Once upon a time…," she started.

"I cannot hear you clearly," said the teacher from the back of the class.

"Once upon a time...," Namukose started again.

"Louder than that."

Namukose looked at the floor.

"Look at me and speak louder, Namukose. You can do it," the teacher encouraged her.

Namukose then narrated what happened to her late Great Grandmother, Kudeba. She said that Kudeba had never been to a hospital in all of her 99 years on this earth. But during her 100th year, she fell ill and was to be taken to hospital. Kudeba had told the relatives that she did not want to go to a place she had never been to before. She had said that if this was to be the end of her life then she would rather die in her small house. The relatives did not listen and decided to carry her to hospital on the bicycle. By bad luck, Kudeba died on the way. Namukose said that she was anointed as the heir to Grandmother Kudeba. Since then, everyone called her 'Grandma', the source of wisdom and advice. She was catapulted to a position of honour and all she wanted was to emulate her grandmother, who was a person who was responsible and cared for others. Namukose said she also hoped to live to be one hundred years without going to hospital!

"Can you clap for her?" Miss Nandase said to the class after Namukose was finished.

The pupils clapped and Namukose ran back to her seat.

That day, when Namukose went back home she asked her mother to teach her more stories. She wanted to be ready the next time she had to tell a story to the class. Mrs Mukose was happy to tell her stories and that evening, while mother and daughter were preparing supper, Namukose's mother told her a story. The story went like this:

Once upon a time, Mrs. Hen and Mrs. Eagle were great friends. They visited each other very often. One day,

Mrs. Hen wanted to mend her children's clothes, so she borrowed a needle from Mrs. Eagle.

"Take care of my needle," said Mrs. Eagle.

"I will do that," Mrs. Hen assured her friend.

While Mrs. Hen was mending her children's clothes, she heard one of the children crying. She placed the needle on the floor and rushed to attend to the baby.

When she came back, she could not see the needle. She looked all over the place but all was in vain. In the afternoon Mrs. Eagle came for her needle. She found her friend busy scratching the ground.

"What are you doing?" she asked.

"I am looking for the needle."

"I told you to be careful with my needle. I want it back right now."

"Give me some more time. I am sure I will find it," Mrs. Hen pleaded.

"I will come back tomorrow," said Mrs. Eagle.

This was a relief to Mrs. Hen. She looked all over the place but could not find the needle.

The following day Mrs. Eagle returned. "Have you found my needle?" she asked.

"Not yet," replied Mrs. Hen.

"If you don't get my needle I will be forced to eat your children one by one."

"You can't do that to me! Give me more time and I will find your needle."

"I give you only tomorrow."

The day after that Mrs. Eagle came back and Mrs. Hen was in tears. She had not yet found the needle.

Mrs. Eagle grabbed one of Mrs. Hen's chicks and went away with it. Since that time, Eagles have been eating chicks and chickens keep on scratching the ground in the hope that one day they will find the needle.

Namukose felt sorry for the chicken. "What a sad story!" she said. "Mum, you have two needles. Can we give one to the chicken?"

This amused her mother very much. "The other one was a special needle. You can only help by protecting the chickens."

That day, Namukose decided that whenever she saw an eagle she would throw a stone at it.

At the end of the year, the pupils had to sit for exams. Namukose's performance was very good. She was the best in Primary One. This made her very happy. The whole school assembled and head teacher Mr Bateganya read out the names of the pupils who had performed very well. The best pupil in each class was given five exercise books and a pencil. In Primary One, Namukose's name was read out. She could not believe her ears. Being the best out of sixty pupils was like a miracle. Mr Bateganya congratulated her and gave her a present. The class teachers gave out the reports to pupils from their respective classes.

Namukose ran all the way home. She could not wait to tell her parents the good news. She found her mother in the kitchen. "I was the best in my class and here are the presents I was given," said Namukose.

"Congratulations, my dear daughter," Mrs. Mukose said, hugging her. "Your father will be happy to hear that."

When Namukose's father, Mukose, came back home from the trading centre that evening, Namukose showed him the report.

And he was very proud. His daughter was the best in the whole class, and she beat both boys and girls. All those who said he was wasting his time sending his girls to school should see this, he thought. "You are as bright as your father," he said, proudly. "Well done!"

He even promised to buy her a school uniform for the next year, when she would be in Primary Two.

Chapter Three

The next year, Bogere, Namukose's younger brother, was six years old and was old enough to join school himself. However, unlike Namukose, Bogere was not excited. It was hard to wake him up in the morning. Namukose shook him hard and called out loudly: ""Wake up, and we go to school!"

He would not budge. "I am still enjoying my sleep," he complained.

"We shall be late for school if you do not wake up," she said, but he would not move. It was only when their mother came in and ordered him to wake up that he finally got out of bed. They rushed to get ready, washed and put on their clothes and ate some breakfast as fast as they could before rushing out of the house. Namukose did not even manage to wear her new uniform smartly. She just pulled on the tunic and ran out of the house.

But on the road, Bogere did not want to walk fast. Namukose urged him to move faster, but he would not. He sulked and dragged his feet. By the time they got to school, the bell had already rung and the teacher on duty was waiting for latecomers.

"Sir, my brother refused to walk fast," Namukose pleaded, but the teacher did not listen to her. Both the children were punished. Namukose was very angry with her brother.

By the time she went to class, the first lesson in math was almost over.

On the opening day of the term, the head teacher usually invited someone to talk to the pupils. This time it was a female dentist. She was smartly dressed in a white gown and a pair of black trousers. Mr Bateganya introduced her to the pupils.

"Good morning, pupils," the dentist said.

"Good morning, madam," the pupils responded.

"The topic today is 'Caring For Our Teeth'." She wrote the words on the blackboard in bold letters for everyone to see.

"How many times do you brush your teeth in a day?" she asked the class.

Some of the pupils raised their hands.

She picked Mukwaya.

"Once a day."

"Who has a different answer?" she asked again.

Other hands went up. This time the dentist picked Nali.

"We are supposed to brush our teeth three times a day."

"Thank you for your answer," the dentist said. "It is good to brush your teeth at least twice a day or more."

Namukose looked at the dentist. She usually brushed her teeth only once a day but this morning she had forgotten to brush them because she was in a hurry to get to school after Bogere had refused to wake up.

But the dentist continued to talk about how to keep teeth healthy and how to look after teeth and the more she spoke, the more Namukose and the other children learnt about dental health. In the end, not only did they want to take good care of their teeth, many of them wanted to be dentists when they grew up. So even though her first day in Primary Two had started badly, it ended well.

The first day set the tone for Primary Two. It came with challenges, but it also had rewards. Namukose had to work hard but she succeeded and passed her exams and in the end, was promoted to Primary Three. Primary Three was different from the past two years because she had to remain at school for afternoon classes. When the bell for lunch rang on the first day of Primary Three, she was hungry and thirsty. There were some boys outside playing football and some girls playing hide-and-seek. She wondered how they managed get the energy to play on an empty stomach.

There was no food and no water to drink at school. While thinking about how thirsty she was, Namukose remembered the pot at home that always had cool water for her. She was very thirsty. The more she thought about it, the more dry her throat seemed. Finally she made up her mind that she was going to go home for lunch. She was sure if she ran she could make it home and back in time for afternoon classes.

She put her books in a corner of the classroom and ran all the way home with her brother, Bogere.

When she got home, her mother had just returned from the garden and was peeling cassava.

"Why have you come back, Namukose?" her mother asked. "Aren't you supposed to have afternoon classes in Primary Three?"

"I have come to eat food," Namukose replied.

"I am sorry food is not ready. Check in the basket for some bananas."

Namukose knew there were no banana. "We had them for breakfast!" she said, sadly.

"Then I have nothing to give you at this time. Food will be ready in a few minutes," her mother said. Her mother had not even put the food on fire yet. Namukose didn't know what to do. She had to get back to school in time for afternoon class. So she gulped down as much water as she could from the pot and ran all the way back to school. The pupils were already in class. The teacher had just finished introducing the lesson.

Namukose knocked on the door. She was tired from her long run and was panting heavily.

"Where have you been?" asked the teacher.

"I had gone home for lunch," she huffed.

"Next time you will be punished for coming to school late. You should be bringing some food in the morning."

Namukose thought seriously. There had been nothing that she could bring. They had had potatoes and green vegetables for supper and there was none left.

Namukose brought out her book and began to write in it. She felt a pang in her stomach and wondered if Primary Three was going to be like at every day.

Little did she know, the teachers were working on making it easier. After school, she was given a letter to take home.

Buwabe P/S
P. O. Box 20
Bugiri

Dear parents,

Re: Meeting

You are hereby invited for a meeting at the above school. It will take place on Friday 7 May at two o'clock.

Keep time.

Yours sincerely,

Mr Bateganya
H/M

Namukose went home and read the letter to her mother, who agreed to attend the meeting.

On Friday, the parents came for the meeting. Namukose's mother arrived on time.

"You are warmly welcome," began the headmaster Mr Bateganya. "We are facing a few problems in the school:

"First of all, we lack accommodation for teachers. As you have seen, we have only two houses. Most of the teachers live three kilometres from school. This makes it difficult for them to keep time.

"Secondly, children have nothing to eat at school. Most of them do not have breakfast and they stay at school on empty stomachs. This affects their ability to learn.

"Lastly, but not least, children report to school late and most of them lack books, pens and uniform. It is your responsibility as parents to provide your children with books, pens, pencils and uniforms. Sending a child to school without books is like a farmer going to dig without a hoe.

"In the eyes of teachers every pupil is special, and that is how they are treated. Let us learn to help ourselves. I leave the floor for you."

One parent rose to his feet. "I am tired of seeing my daughter sent home because she doesn't have a mere pencil," he complained. "She should be given the chance to stay at school while I look for money to buy whatever she needs."

"That would be a good idea, but when they have nothing to do they end up disturbing everyone," replied Mr Bateganya.

Another parent stood up, and said, "My son has a new pair of shorts and a shirt. Is it necessary to buy a uniform for him?"

"It is necessary for you to buy a uniform. In case of a problem it is easy for the child to be identified and the school can be informed quickly."

Another parent complained, "Children have to report to school at sunrise and return home at sunset. There is a lot that needs to be done at home and as parents we need the children's help."

"That will be looked into," responded Mr Bateganya.

"Children are given a lot of homework. They are at school for the greater part of the day. But this homework is a daily thing. When do they find time to rest?" asked another parent.

"Homework is good for the children but the teachers shall give a reasonable amount of homework in each subject."

Another parent complained, "Some of us have ulcers and we have not yet had lunch. Could you please wind up?"

This amused the headmaster. He laughed gently before he answered," That is how the children feel. Young as they are, they try to put on a brave face. So what should we do to provide lunch for these children?"

A lady raised her hand.

"Yes madam," Mr Bateganya said.

"We should contribute money," the lady said.

A man shot up. "I do not agree with what she is saying," he said. "She talks about money as if it is easy to get. How much does she have herself?"

"Give her a chance to talk," said Mr Bateganya.

"I suggest we contribute three thousand shillings per child per term," said the lady.

"Money is difficult to come by for some of us," he said. "Can we contribute a few kilos of maize instead?"

"That is also a good idea, and since it is nearing harvest time it will be easy to provide the maize," put in Mr Bateganya.

The meeting went on to discuss how the food and money would be collected and organised and it ended on a happy note. Something was going to be done to save the children from having to try to study on empty stomachs.

Each parent would bring three thousand shillings or three kilogrammes of maize for each pupil. The Feeding Programme Committee collected the food and money and soon the pupils would have their first meal at school.

Everybody was excited. The first meal was a success. They pupils didn't have to run home in order to have something to eat. They had time to rest. Others played games energetically. The boys played football. Namukose skipped rope with her friends. She was happy that she would not have to worry about pangs of hunger any more.

To supplement the food and money from the feeding programme, Mr Bateganya decided to start a school garden. One of the villagers was ready to lend the school a piece of land which the children could cultivate so that they could grow some food to eat. Some parents donated bean and maize seeds.

Not only did the children get a better diet in the end, they also had the opportunity to learn about agriculture and how to have a balanced diet.

Namukose liked it when the agriculture teacher took the class out to the farm. There was fresh air outside, gardening with her friends was fun, plus it was good exercise and it is a rest from difficult things like mathematics.

The teacher split the class up in groups and gave each group a task. The students began to talk amongst themselves as they worked.

"Some people get a lot of money from their farms," said Kabugudhe.

"Who are those?" Kayale asked

"There is a man in our village called Muggaga. He grows vegetables and rears animals at the same time. The whole village buys vegetables and milk from him. He is rich!" Kabugudhe said.

"I think I will also be a farmer," said Kayale. "I also want to be rich when I grow up."

"That is interesting," said the teacher. "If you want to be a successful farmer you have to pay attention to the lessons I teach you here. You will learn good methods of farming like mulching, crop rotation and how to make fertilisers. You will also have to work hard. Remember, you cannot succeed unless you work hard."

The pupils took what the teacher said to heart and they worked hard in the farm. They sang songs and helped each other in all the tasks and soon it was harvest time.

Everyone was very excited when they finally got to harvest what they had spent so long growing. Namukose and her friends uprooted the first cassava with glee. It was so big!

They knew it would be delicious when they finally got to eat it for lunch along with all the other food they had harvested.

When the teacher saw the children laugh and smile as they danced around the cassava, he was very happy and proud of them.

The feeding programme at Buwabe Primary School was successful and the news of it spread like a bushfire. Soon pupils were leaving other schools to join Buwabe. The classes were getting full. The teachers were worried. They ran to the headmaster to complain.

A group of teachers got together and marched to the headmaster's office to talk to him. They found him seated in his small office with an elderly European gentleman. The two men were talking keenly about something, and the teachers at first thought they should wait outside, but Mr Bateganya looked up and saw them.

"Dr Paige, these are my teachers," he said, indicating the teachers outside.

"They look like they have something on their minds," said Dr Paige, smiling at the teachers. "I will let you deal with that issue then we can continue our discussion."

They shook hands and Mr Bateganya walked out to meet the teachers.

Miss Nandase did not waste any time. She immediately stated the problem.

"Mr Bateganya, there are too many children in our classrooms. We don't have enough seats for all of them!" she said. "Some of the pupils are sitting on the floor!"

The headmaster knew that there had been many new children coming to join the school, but he calmed the agitated teachers down. "Do not worry," he said. "These children are hungry for education. We cannot turn them away. We have to allow them to join us. We shall find a solution to the shortage of seats in the long run."

The teacher looked at him for a long time. She decided that he should see it for himself.

"Sir, you should come to my class and see what is going on," she said.

When Mr Bateganya got to the class a few minutes later, he was shocked. The classroom was so full that even the teachers had little space to move about. Each desk had five pupils trying to share it and those were the lucky ones. The unlucky ones sat on the floor.

"Teacher, Mataayo is pushing us," complained one of the pupils loudly. The room was so crowded that the pupils had not even realised that head teacher was in class.

Mr Bateganya coughed loudly and said, "Good morning, class."

The students struggled to get up so that they could greet the headmaster standing, but those who were sitting on the floor almost couldn't get up.

Miss Nandase looked at Mr Bateganya. "This is the situation we are in," she said. "How can they learn to write well when they are seated on the floor? They keep rolling on the floor and dirt gets into their books and uniforms."

Mr Bateganya was shocked! He had not imagined that the situation was that bad. But he could not send the children away. They also needed to get an education.

Miss Nandase called on Namukose and asked her to bring out her book. "Lucy Namukose is one of our best pupils," the teacher said to the headmaster. "Look at her book."

The paper had turned brown. There were patches of dirt all over the book, from the days when she missed a chance to sit at the desk and had to sit on the floor.

"Pupils like Namukose are eager to learn under whatever circumstances, but it is very difficult when the class is so full."

The headmaster held his chin in his hand and shook his head. This was a big problem.

Suddenly he had an idea. "Tell the children to bring some mats or stools, or whatever else they can find at home that they can use to sit on. This will alleviate the problem until we can find a better solution," he said. He was still holding his chin in his hand when he turned around to go back to his office, still thinking of the problem. It would take ages to get the government to build a new classroom. The school could not do it – the school did not have enough money either. What about the parents? But this was a poor rural village. The families were struggling to get school uniforms and stationery for their children. They would never be able to raise enough for an entire school block.

The headmaster walked all the way back to his office thinking about this problem.

But in half an hour he was back outside the classroom smiling from ear to ear. He waved Miss Nandase out of the crowded class eagerly. Seeing the expression on his face, she moved quickly. "What is it, Mr Bateganya?" she asked once she was outside the door.

Once outside she could see that the head teacher was not alone. The European visitor from his office was with him. "Dr Paige, please tell her the good news, so that it can relieve her anxiety."

The elderly man smiled. "Madam, I represent a church in Britain. I am here looking for worthy charitable causes our church can support. I need to go back and file a report, but if it works out, then I am sure my church would love to build you two new classrooms!"

Miss Nandase could barely contain her joy. Mr Bateganya had to remind her to keep it down.

However two months later, she was able to release her joy. She cheered the loudest at the official opening of two new classroom blocks donated by the Church of Saint Stephen in Sheffield, UK. Dr Paige was very shocked when she gave him a special hug at the opening ceremony, and Namukose, who was selected to offer Dr Paige a wreath of flowers as the guest of honour, laughed to herself to see the look of surprise on his face.

In the new, more spacious classrooms it was easier to pay attention in class and easier to learn. Namukose sat near the front, where the windows let in plenty of light and she listened closely to the teacher. On this day her health teacher, Miss Sanyu, was teaching the class about water and how to make it safe to drink. It was not good to drink water that was not boiled, Miss Sanyu had said. When the teacher said that Namukose immediately remembered how many times she had drank spring water and got stomach pain. And all she had to do was boil the water to make it safe! She was glad this was not a crowded class! If she had been hidden at the back of a crowd of children, she might not have heard that.

When she got home that evening she would tell her parents. Both her father and mother were sitting outside the house when she returned. "Mummy, daddy, guess what they taught us at school today!" she called cheerfully from the distance, as she ran towards the house.

Mr Mukose smiled when he saw her. He was now proud of his daughter who was doing well in school. He welcomed her with a hug and asked, "What did my clever girl learn today?"

"Our science teacher taught us that we should always boil our drinking water," Namukose said to her father.

"But why?" Mrs. Mukose asked.

"It is because water might have germs," Namukose replied. "Boiling it kills them."

"You know very well that we do not have enough firewood to cook food," said her mother, sounding tired. "Where are we going to get firewood for boiling water daily?"

"The teacher said we can put a kettle on to the fire after preparing meals, so we don't need to get more firewood every time." Namukose explained.

Her father patted her shoulder. "That is a clever idea.

It saves on firewood," he said. Namukose continued. "The teacher also advised us to wash our hands with soap after using the toilet."

Mrs Mukose spoke sadly again. "My dear daughter, your demands are becoming very many. We are poor. It is already hard enough for us to get a piece of soap to wash our clothes. Where shall we get soap for washing our hands all the time?"

"The teacher told us that it is for our own good," continued the little girl. "There are lots of germs in the latrine that are dangerous to our lives. If we do not wash our hands they will make us sick. He also advised us to use latrines and make covers for them to keep away flies that might contaminate our food,"

"Well, that is a good idea. We shall try to follow your teacher's advice," said Mrs Mukose.

Namukose was very happy that she had convinced her parents and they would not suffer from diseases like typhoid that could be avoided. She was encouraged to continue using her knowledge from school to help at home. Not only did she help her mother to learn how to read also she made her father proud.

Chapter Four

One of the ways in which Namukose helped her parents at home was through reading and writing. They were glad about this. Her mother often told her how happy she was that she had someone at home to write letters. "Before this whenever we had a letter to write, we had to go to the chief's office, and tell him what to put in the letter. There was no way of keeping privacy. He knew all our secrets!"

One day in school, the teachers showed her how to write a friendly letter. Until then, the only reading and writing she had done had been for grown up things for her parents, or school issues. Now she was going to learn how to write for fun!

The teacher told all the pupils to write a letter to their friends in other schools nearby. Namukose wondered who to write to. Then she remembered her friend Kasubo.

She got down to write the letter. She wrote:

> Buwabe Primary School
> P. O. Box 20
> Bugiri

Dear Kasubo,

I am pleased to write to you this letter. How are you?

How do you find school? This way we are fine and we have just learnt how to write a letter. Shall we meet over the weekend so that we play? Let me hope that this letter finds you well.

Your friend,

Lucy Namukose

All the pupils who wrote letters handed them to the teacher. The teacher the sorted them out according to which of the four neighbouring schools they were going to. Kasubo's letter was on top of the small pile of letters that were going to her school. Namukose prayed hard that she would receive it soon. Kasubo would be so surprised, thought Namukose.

Sure enough, the next day at break time at Kasubo's school on the other side of the hill, a pile of letters arrived from the Primary Five class of Namukose's school.

Kasubo and her friends were very puzzled when the teacher called them over and gave them letters. They had assumed that the letters were for their teachers. When the teacher gave them the envelopes, they thought the letters were for their parents. When they saw their names on the envelopes, they were very excited.

Kasubo was so happy with her letter from Namukose that she read it over and over again. When the bell rang for class, Kasubo was still reading the letter. She even went into class with it.

In Kasubo's classroom, Namulinda, the girl who sat behind her, wanted to have a look at the letter. She begged, but Kasubo refused to give it to her.

Namulinda decided to do something mean. She put up her hand and said to the teacher, "Excuse me, sir. Kasubo has got a letter from her boyfriend!"

The whole class was shocked. What? They all gasped.

"Can I have that letter?" the teacher demanded.

Kasubo frowned at Namulinda as she walked to the front of the class. She handed the letter over to the teacher. All the other pupils were looking at each other, wondering what the teacher was going to do to her.

The teacher took the letter and looked at it. He read it and then said, "Hmm. Kasubo, you should put this letter away now. It is time for class. You will reply to it in your free time, okay?"

Kasubo put the letter in her pocket and went back to her seat. Namulinda meanwhile was steaming with jealousy!

One Friday morning at Namukose's school, when the teacher walked into class, he was not prepared for the sight that met his eyes. There was hardly anyone there. Half of the seats were empty! "Where are all the pupils?" he wondered.

"Where are your classmates, children?" he asked the few pupils who were in the class. They looked at him in wonder. Didn't the teacher know what day it was?

"Teacher, they have gone to the market. It is market day today," they replied.

"Oh," said the teacher. He had forgotten that it was market day. On market day everyone in the village who had anything to sell would go out to the market to try and find a buyer, and those who needed to buy something would go to the market to find it. The villagers would meet at the market to trade in foodstuffs and in other things like clothes, soap, salt and so on. The children also went along because children often had something to do on market day. Parents usually needed their help carrying goods around.

But even if there was a lot of work to do on market day, what about education? The children needed to be in school, not out at the market. The teacher could not teach a half empty class!

He returned to the teachers' room perplexed, only to find that the other teachers were complaining of the same thing.

"What are we going to do to reduce absenteeism on market day?" one of the teachers asked another. "Half of my class has not turned up."

"It's the same problem in my class," said the other teacher.

"What is the draw of market day?" asked one of the new teachers. "What sort of things are sold in the market?"

"Things like food, old clothes and new clothes, and so on," another teacher answered.

"I need a blanket for my child," said the new teacher. "I might as well go and buy one."

The new teacher gave up on trying to stay behind to teach his half-empty class and left to go to the market, leaving the other teachers to puzzle over his behaviour.

Namukose did not go to school that market day either. She took a mat she had made to the market. She managed to sell it. She brought the money back and shared it with her mother.

"Now we shall be able to buy salt and soap," her mother had said.

Even though she was one of the first pupils to arrive at school the following Monday, Namusoke still had to explain her absence the previous week.

"Namukose," the teacher taking the roll-call called out her name.

"Present sir," she responded.

"Where were you on Friday?" asked the teacher

She did not know what to tell him.

"Have you heard my question?" the teacher asked.

"Yes sir."

"Where were you on Friday?"

"Sir, I went to the market to sell my mat."

"Couldn't your parents do that for you?" the teacher asked, sternly.

Namukose did not know how to answer that question. The truth was a long story.

It started when the pupils were introduced to practical skills. The teachers came in to teach them how to make pots out of clay and how to make brooms and mats from materials that were available around the school and around their homes.

"You can sell your handicrafts and get money," the teacher had said. This excited the pupils a great deal.

Namukose had been enjoying the classes very much, and had written notes very carefully. Soon she found that her books were getting full and her pens were getting empty. She would need new books and pens very soon!

When she got home that evening she told her mother about her problem. "Where do these school people expect us to get money for books all the time? Let us wait. Maybe your father will get them for you."

Every day Mukose would go to town very early in the morning and return home late in the evening. When he returned that evening, his wife told him that the children needed new books and pens.

"Where am I going to get money from?" he asked.

"But Dad, you always go to town. We thought you had a job there," said Namukose, innocently.

"Children of these days have no manners at all. Who gave you permission to ask me what I do in town? What do you expect me to do at home? Cook for you? I am busy and I have many things to do. You should learn not to ask questions like that to your father!" he snapped, and then stomped off in a rage.

But Namukose was upset. She did not want to go to school without any pens and books. Then she remembered what the teacher had said. She said that they could make money from selling mats and brooms they made from the reeds and grass around their homes. Namukose had a brilliant idea.

She ran to her mother. "Mummy I have a good idea," she said.

"What idea is that?" her mother asked.

"We can make money by weaving baskets and mats."

"I do not know how to weave mats."

"I will teach you, Mummy. We learnt it at school and our teacher said we could make money by selling our products."

"That is a good idea. We shall collect the palm leaves on our way to the well."

They collected the palm leaves from the nearby bushes, carried them home and spread them out to dry. When the leaves had dried, Namukose and her mother started weaving mats. This occupied them the whole weekend. When the mats were big enough, and when Mr Mukose saw them, he agreed to take them to town with him and sell them for a good price. This made Namukose very happy and from the moment her father rode off in the morning, with the mats strapped to the back of his bicycle, she was filled with anxiety. She could not wait for him to come back with the books and pens that had been bought with the money from her very own handiwork. She felt so grown up!

When her father returned in the evening, there was no mat on the bicycle. But Namukose's heart sank when she saw that there was no package of books on his bicycle either.

"Did you manage to sell the mats, daddy?" she asked.

"Yes, I did. I managed to use the money to pay a man in town whose debt I had. He had been bothering me very much. Now I can relax," said Mr Mukose. He pushed his bicycle past her and went off to look for her mother. He wanted his supper.

Namukose felt like crying. She was so disappointed. All that work and she still did not have exercise books!

Still, she had no choice. She was determined to get money for her exercise books. She went out and gathered more papyrus and got down to work, making another mat. She worked at it for hours. When it was finally finished, she carried it to the market herself and sold it. Then she was able to buy books and pens at last.

When the teacher asked her why she was not at school on market day, she could not tell him that long story. When he asked why her parents couldn't sell the mat for her, she said, "My parents were busy."

"When you sold the mat what did you use the money for?"

"I bought exercise books and pens."

The teacher looked at her and did not know what to do. At first he could not decide whether to congratulate her for showing that she cared about her education, or to punish her for not attending school.

Then he decided to leave her alone. "Sit down," he said. He knew that Namukose was a good girl and a good student.

Not only did Namukose work hard at school, she also had a lot of work to do afterwards. In addition to her homework, there were household chores to perform. She tried to do everything she had to do on time. She fetched water and cleaned the home, and did all the things her mother told her to do, then she settled down to do her homework.

It was already dark on this night, so she had to find a lamp to give her enough light to do her work.

As she walked into the store to find a lamp, she passed her brother Bogere, who had just come back from a long game of football. He was dirty and his shorts were covered in dust. He had been playing all evening. He had not even collected water from the well, which meant that he was not even going to be able to take a bath that night. But he didn't care, because no one was going to scold him about it. It annoyed Namukose very much. "Why does he get away with everything he does?" she asked herself. "Even if he comes home late no one asks him where he has been!" It was always different for boys, it seemed. They always seemed to be treated better than the girls.

Bogere ran past her without saying anything to her and he disappeared into the house. Namukose continued to the store. When she got there, after rummaging through the dark, she finally found a lamp. She picked up the small wick lamp, put it to her ear and shook it. There was no sound. The tin lamp did not have any paraffin.

"How am I going to do my homework tonight?" she said aloud to herself. "What will I tell the teacher?"

The next day everybody handed in their homework when the teacher asked, but Namukose did not. She just looked at the teacher. When the teacher walked over to her, he asked, "Can I have your book?"

"I did not do the homework."

"Why?"

"There was no paraffin at home," she replied.

"Why didn't you buy any?" the teacher asked.

"We didn't have the money, sir," Namukose said, looking down in shame.

The teacher felt sorry for her. At first he didn't know what to say. It wasn't her fault. Then he spoke. "Make sure you do it at break-time," he said.

When the bell rang for break, Namukose remained seated at her desk.

"Aren't you coming out to play with us?" asked one of the pupils.

"Not now. I have to do my homework," Namukose responded.

The other children went out and played all through the break, while Namukose sat at her desk, hunched over her books, trying to fill in the answers. She could hear the noise of laughter as the other pupils played football or jumped rope or played ball. They were having so much fun. She wished she could join them. Even Bogere was out there playing football again. All he ever did, it seemed, was play football.

Namukose began to think about how much she wished she could also just play all the time. But then she remembered sharply that she was not supposed to be thinking such thoughts. She had to finish her homework. She turned her eyes away from the windows and looked squarely at the books, and began to attack the questions the teacher had set for homework.

It was when Namukose was in Primary Five that her periods started. One morning her clothes felt wet. She thought she wanted to go to the bathroom so she asked for permission from the teacher.

"Excuse me teacher, may I go outside?" she said.

"Yes, you may," the teacher said.

Namukose stood up and ran outside. Her dress was stained. Some of the other pupils who saw the stain as she ran outside started to laugh. The teacher was busy writing on the blackboard so she did not see the stain. She wondered why the pupils were laughing.

"What is amusing you children?" she asked.

The pupils fell silent. The teacher insisted, "What is going on?"

There was no answer.

"Will you leave my class if you are not ready to tell me what you are laughing at?"

One of the pupils put up her hand. When the teacher picked him, he said, "They are laughing at Namukose whose dress has been stained."

"Laughing at her is a sign of ignorance. Never make fun of girls again," she warned them.

The teacher saw the stain also and immediately understood what was happening. She walked out of the classroom with Namukose and placed her hand on the young girl's shoulder and began to explain. "Namukose, what is happening is called menstruation. It is natural for girls to have it once a month. It occurs to every woman and girl of a certain age. They should not laugh at you."

Namukose was comforted, but was still confused. So the teacher took her to the nurse, who provided her with sanitary towels and told her all about periods and what they meant. In the end, Namukose felt better. She was less puzzled. In fact, she was even proud that she was becoming a woman. At the end of the day, she could not wait to break the news to her mother.

"Mama, I have news for you," she said.

"What news do you have for me, my daughter?'

"I have started my monthly periods."

Her mother was happy, but had some strong advice to give her. "You should learn to be clean. Bathe at least two times a day and change your pads regularly. You should also be very careful with boys now."

This worried Namukose. How careful should she be with the boys? In class, she shared a desk with boys. Does it mean it was not good to sit with boys?

"You should not allow anybody to play with your private parts," her mother warned.

This amused Namukose. Why should anyone want to play with my private parts? she asked herself.

Soon Namukose's periods stopped and she was able to feel comfortable again. She knew that she would have to manage them carefully every month, but was proud because that meant that she was now a woman.

It was a cool evening after school one day a few weeks later, and Namukose and her mother were working in the kitchen. Namusoke turned to her mother and asked what the two of them, being the women of the house, were going to do for women's day, now that Namukose knew she was a woman. Her mother had to ask. "What is Women's Day, Namukose?"

"Tomorrow is Women's Day," she told her Mother.

"What happens on that day?" her mother asked. "Do women get a holiday from their duties like cooking, fetching water, sweeping the house and so on?"

"It is the day women are recognised for the good job they do," Namukose said.

"Even the rural women like me?"

"Of course. There are going to be celebrations in town to mark the day. We should attend them."

"What is there to celebrate? We are still doing the work our parents did. We fetch water from the well in big pots with our children strapped on our backs. We grind millet on grinding stones. We live in grass-thatched houses and sleep on the floor like animals," Namukose's mother said with a weary voice.

"But we have to celebrate women's achievements all over the world," Namukose said. "Our teacher told us that the other year, for the first time ever, a woman was elected as a president in Africa. She is from Liberia. That is very good news for the women. In our own country we had a woman Vice President and we have many women representing us in Parliament. Since many girls go to school now, our teacher says life for women will change for the better. Women will be able to support themselves. They will have control over their own lives and take important decisions on what concerns them. Mummy, we should go to the celebrations and see what they say there."

It sounded like a good idea to Mrs Mukose. She wanted to know what was going on. What her daughter had said was interesting. "Okay, we shall go tomorrow. But today, let us finish our work. We can celebrate afterwards."

The function was in town the next day. Many women and girls gathered in the churchyard in town. Some had dressed well for the day, but others just wore their normal clothes. Some mothers carried their children on their backs while others breast-fed theirs. Some men also attended. There was a large crowd but Jane Mukose felt that most of them were like her: they had come out of curiosity, not because they fully understood the purpose of the celebrations.

But they soon got to see what it was all about when the guest of honour arrived. It was a woman. She arrived in a white Mitsubishi Pajero. She was riding in the back while a young man in front drove the car for her. She was smartly dressed in a nice gomesi. She got out of the car and walked confidently to a table that had been arranged in the shade beneath a tree. LC Chairman Bukenya smiled happily when she arrived and called on everybody to clap for her to show their welcome. He introduced her with pride as a very important person, the head of a whole faculty in Makerere University. "She is a daughter of this area, and she represents us well in Kampala. We should all be very proud of her. Ladies and Gentlemen, please welcome Dr Robina Kalembe.

"I would like to thank Chairman Bukenya, and all the people of this area for inviting, me," she said, beginning her speech. "We are here to celebrate, but we must not rest. We as women do a lot of work, and we are here to celebrate and recognise the efforts of our mothers and our daughters. But we must not rest yet. There is still a lot of work to be done in the community."

Dr Kalembe paused to look at everybody. Then she continued. "Most of our homes are not as clean as they should be. Some of you do not have latrines. The paths going to your houses are bushy. Most of you are reluctant to seek medical care in time, especially the women. You have to ask for permission from your husbands to go to hospital for treatment. If the permission is not given, you stay at home. This has cost us a lot of lives. Ladies, you should try to make some money for yourselves so that you can take care of yourselves. There is a lot you can do, like making handicrafts, growing vegetables and rearing chickens. It is important to have something you can sell instead of relying on others. Make sure you take your children to school. I hope by next year you will all have done something to improve your lives."

She said many other things after that, most of them connected with the concerns of women and the areas in which women had made reasonable progress.

Jane Mukose listened to all of it keenly. It was all very interesting and gripping to hear this woman talk about things she had thought about for a long time. Namukose saw the look in her mother's eye and smiled because she knew how her mother was feeling. That is how Namukose also felt in school. She loved to learn because she knew it would help her have a better life, and help her make the lives of others better, too.

After the function they both went home talking about what Dr Kalembe had said. She had given them many ideas on how to improve their homes and earn extra income so that they would not have to depend on their husbands for everything. Namukose agreed with that a lot. She had already learnt that by making mats she could get money to buy her own books.

They reached home to find Mr Mukose waiting for them. He was angry.

"Where have you been?" he asked.

"I have been in town attending Women's Day celebrations," Jane Mukose replied.

"Who gave you permission to go to town?" he asked. "Have you forgotten your place?"

"Which is my place?" asked Mrs Musoke.

"The kitchen. Those celebrations are for women who have little to do. You, on the other hand, have a lot on your hands. Where is my supper? You should know that you were brought to this house to cook for me, to look after my children and to obey me always. You should not starve me when I grow all the food."

Mr Mukose was furious. He was waving his hands around wildly and shouting very loudly. Namukose's mother was frightened. She moved away from him. "I will make something quickly for you to eat," she said, and she began to edge into the kitchen. As she boiled some water to make millet bread to serve with fish for her husband, she looked over at her daughter. The pride and happiness that she had felt at the Women's Day celebrations were gone. But Namukose could sense a message in her eyes. Her mother looked at her as if to say, "My daughter, make sure you work very hard at school. Get an education so that you can have a better life. I want you to be like Dr Kalembe, don't end up like this."

Chapter Five

It was time to elect new school prefects when Namukose returned to school, and, with the words of Dr Robinah Kalembe still in her heart, Namukose was determined to stand for elections. She had seen that a woman could also be in a position of power and that she could use this position to help others, especially women. When she returned to school, she gave her name to the headmaster and immediately set about campaigning for the post of Head Prefect.

She campaigned hard. "If you vote for me, I will make sure I serve you," she told her fellow students. She was very well-liked in the school, and many of her friends also campaigned for her, telling their friends to tell their friends to vote for her. When the time for voting came, the pupils had to line up behind the candidate they supported.

The teachers counted the pupils, but even without counting it could be seen that the longest line was behind Namukose. Most of the girls supported her, but there were many boys in her line as well. The majority of the school's pupils wanted her to be their head prefect. She was announced the winner and her supporters cheered wildly. Two strong girls carried her around the school. She was very happy. She was ready to play an important role in the lives of her fellow pupils.

The prefects were sworn in by head teacher Mr Bateganya. All the teachers and the pupils cheered them.

For her first task as Head Prefect, Namukose called a meeting of the girls in the school. She wanted to know the problems they faced so that she could help them. She knew that there were many problems that affected them that did not affect the boys. She met them at break time and greeted them.

"We only have a short time, because we have to go back to class after break. But I am here to listen to the problems you face. Please put up your hand if you have anything to tell us."

"Boys laugh at us in class," a girl in Primary Five said, putting up her hand.

"That is true. They make fun of us," another girl said. "If you give a wrong answer to any question asked by the teacher the boys laugh at you."

Namukose wrote this down.

"Others pinch us on our way home," said another girl. "As for me, when it is time to go out for break, the others, especially the boys, push me around," said another.

"We do not have a place to bathe," said a girl in Primary six. By now the girls were not putting up their hands and waiting to be chosen. It seems there were so many problems that they all wanted to make sure they said their piece before they ran out of time. One of Namukose's friends, Nabirye, shouted from the back of the group, "I was nicknamed 'Jaaja' because I have big breasts!"

Namukose just tried to make sure she wrote down everything that was being said.

In a short while, the bell rang for class. The girls were still clamoring to voice their problems. Namukose, as a girl herself, had known that there were many problems, but even she had not expected such a commotion at the meeting. She had to calm the girls down and remind them that it was time for class.

"I have written all your problems down. They are all noted," she said, above the noise. "Thank you for coming to this meeting. I am going to give this information to the Senior Woman Teacher. We will find solutions to all these problems."

The girls cheered their new Head Prefect as they dispersed to return to their classrooms.

Namukose met the Senior Woman Teacher after school lunch. They sat in her classroom and talked. "I see the problem of the bathing, and problems like that are separate. We shall discuss these ones later. The main problem here

42

is that the girls are being laughed at by the boys, or they are being teased or bullied. We cannot allow this. I will talk to Mr Bateganya about it immediately," she said. Namukose was glad that her work was moving so fast.

The following day there was a staff meeting. It was resolved that the whole school should be addressed at assembly. It was also resolved that the pupils who bullied their schoolmates should be warned and their parents informed about their bad behaviour. The teachers and the children had to be on the lookout for such children who intimidated others.

The staff meeting ended at midday. The head teacher ordered one of the pupils to ring the bell and call the whole school for assembly. The pupils were surprised to hear the bell.

"We are going to have lunch early," a pupil commented.

"Why do you think of food all the time?" another pupil said.

"Maybe they are going to introduce a new teacher to us."

"Hurry up," said the class teacher, guiding her pupils out of class to the assembly area.

The pupils stood in straight lines in their respective classes. They were more attentive than ever.

"Good afternoon, all of you," greeted the head teacher.

"Good afternoon, sir," responded the pupils.

"I have called you at this time because I am not happy with some of you," he continued.

The pupils looked at each other. Others held their breath, praying that they were not among the pupils who had angered the headmaster.

"It has come to our knowledge that some pupils bully others. We are not going to entertain that sort of behaviour in this school. I have a list of pupils who intimidate others, so if you hear your name read come forward," the headmaster continued.

There was total silence. The headmaster read out the names. One by one the pupils whose names were called stood in front of the whole school.

"What are they going to do to them?" asked one of the pupils.

"They are going to punish them."

"I mean what punishment are they going to give them?"

"Let us wait and see."

"In front of you are some very bad boys," said Mr Bateganya. "They abuse girls, pinch them, and chase them on their way home. They bully other girls in various ways. We are not going to tolerate children who make life difficult for others." Pointing a finger at them, he said, "This is the last warning I am giving you. If your name comes to me again for bullying, I will expel you from this school."

All the pupils looked at the boys.

"Did you hear that?" one of the boys told his neighbour. "They might be sent away from school. That is very serious."

"You should all be on the lookout for such children who make life hell for others," Mr Bateganya said. "Report them to the teachers or come straight to my office and we shall deal with them accordingly. Where is the Head Prefect?"

Everybody thought she was going to be punished.

"I would like to thank the Head Prefect for letting us know some of the problems you have been facing. Can you clap for her?"

Namukose stood up and bowed to the school, but she knew that the work was not yet done. There were other problems that still needed attention.

And sure enough, the Senior Woman Teacher did not disappoint Namukose. Within a week the school had set up a plan for the bathrooms. The children were told to bring materials for building bath shelters from home. Some brought mats and papyrus. Others brought reeds, stones and poles. Then the children, under the guidance of the teachers, went about putting up bathing structures in the corner of the school compound. They were not difficult to build and in a few hours there were three bathrooms for boys and three for girls. The school brought basins and some soap, so now the pupils were able to bathe at school. The girls were very happy. Some of them had been staying at home during the difficult days of their menstrual cycles because there was no place for them to have a bath.

Namukose was happy to see that she had played a part in improving on the well-being of the pupils. But that was not all. Her list had got the woman teachers thinking and they had written to the district education headquarters to see if there was a way of getting free sanitary towels. In the afternoon, the day after the bathrooms were built, the Senior Woman Teacher called all the big girls from Primary Five and above. They wondered what she was going to tell them. She taught them about how to maintain body hygiene.

Then an official from the district headquarters came to the school. He had some boxes in his car. The pupils were anxious to see what was in the boxes. The boxes were handed over to the Senior Woman Teacher. She gave out packets of sanitary towels.

"What are these for?" asked one of the girls.

The Senior Woman Teacher opened one of the packets and explained to them how what they contained was to be used.

The girls felt very happy as they went back to their classes.

"What is in those packets?" asked one of the boys.

"That is the kind of curiosity that killed a cat," responded one of the girls.

"We also want them," shouted another boy.

This amused the girls.

"Hey, are you crazy? They are not for boys."

There was commotion in the class.

"What is all the noise about?" asked the teacher.

"We also want those packets," some of the boys shouted.

"Those are sanitary towels and they are for girls only," explained the teacher.

At the end of the day the girls could not wait to go home to tell their parents and siblings the good news.

When she arrived back home, Namukose showed her mother the packets.

"What are these for?" her mother asked.

Namukose explained to her.

"You are a lucky girl," her mother remarked. "Now that is one problem solved. Nothing will stop you from going to school anymore."

Namukose was lucky, but she was soon to find out that not everyone was as lucky as her. On one weekend she went to visit her neighbour and schoolmate, Namaganda, who lived nearby. Namaganda was in the class above Namukose at school, but they were almost the same age and had been friends for all their lives.

The two girls talked for a while in Namaganda's family compound before her mother called Namaganda in. There was a visitor to see her.

It was her aunt Kyotasibye. Namaganda was quite excited to see her.

"Come nearer," said her aunt. "You have grown into a beautiful girl. Look at your breasts now. They are bigger than mine when I was your age."

Namaganda didn't know what to say to this. She looked at her mother. "Your aunt has interesting news for you," Maama Namaganda said.

Namaganda thought that her aunt had perhaps bought her a new dress. "I can't wait to hear it," she said.

Auntie Kyotasibye smiled broadly. "Guess what: I got you a rich, hard-working man to get married to," she told Namaganda.

Namaganda caught her breath. Namukose, couldn't believe it.

"I am too young to get married," Namaganda protested.

"Do not say that," her aunt responded. "Look at me. I got married at fourteen. You are already fifteen. You will be happy if you get married now. Many girls never get this kind of chance."

Instead of looking happy, Namaganda started crying.

"Do not bother crying, my daughter," the aunt said, "because it will not change anything. Your mother and I have already decided that you will get married immediately, and the rich man we have chosen for you will be coming here tomorrow."

Namaganda turned to her mother, trying to choke back her tears.

"Mama I still want to continue going to school. We learn a lot there and I do not want to miss my friends." Namaganda wept loudly as she spoke.

"You have no choice in the matter. Your future husband is coming soon. You should get used to the idea. Now go outside with your friend. Me and your aunt have things to discuss," said her mother sternly.

Namaganda felt helpless. She felt that there was no one to turn to. She walked out of the house sobbing and clutching Namukose for comfort. Namukose did not know what to say, so she started to cry, too.

Meanwhile, back in the Mukose home, far from getting her out of school, her mother was trying to convince her father to give her more time there. Namukose's class teacher had requested them to give Namukose enough time to concentrate on her studies. They had suggested that the work at home be shared by Bogere.

"That is between you and your daughter," Mukose said. "As far as I am concerned, domestic chores are for women and girls. I am more interested in what the teacher thinks about Bogere. What did the teacher say about him?"

"All his teachers say that he is playful in class."

"What do they expect us to do?"

"We have to discipline him," said Mrs. Mukose.

"That is the work of the teachers. They should discipline him themselves."

"The teacher said we have to work together to help him."

"Is that all?" he asked.

"We have to attend meetings together next time," said Mrs. Mukose.

"What are you saying? Do you know the number of times teachers invite us for meetings? They invite us for meetings all the time. These meetings never end. That means we shall not have time to do anything for ourselves. You have to attend meetings alone. There is no way I can miss out on my work in town."

Mrs Mukose knew that Mukose did not really have a job in town, but she did not say anything.

Namaganda's marriage saddened Namukose. All girls wanted to get married, she supposed. Namukose also dreamt about getting married and having a family. But she wanted to find a husband only after completing her studies and getting a job. She did not want to be like her mother, who worked so hard on the farm but was not allowed to sell anything, while her father did nothing all day long.

Chapter Six

After six years of hard work, Namukose eventually joined Primary Seven. The pupils in Primary Seven liked to be called 'candidates' or 'leavers', because they were candidates for Primary Leaving Examinations. They walked with pride in their position.

But it was not all puffed chests. There was a lot of work on their hands. The class teacher was a very strict man. They had to report to school very early in the morning and attend an extra lesson before the rest of the pupils. This meant Namukose had to wake up even earlier in the morning so that she could dig in the farm and fetch water before going to school.

Moreover, she had to carry very many books to school. Every day the number of books she had to take to school increased in number. Namukose did not have a school bag. She used polythene bags. Her hands would often hurt from carrying the heavy bags.

One day Namukose didn't return home from school on time. Her mother waited and waited, but Namukose was nowhere to be seen.

"What is this girl up to?" she wondered.

Her brother had not returned either but this did not bother Mrs Mukose. She knew that Bogere, like all boys, liked to stop to play football on the way home from school.

When Namukose finally arrived, her mother asked her angrily: "Where have you been?"

"I am coming from school," she answered.

"What type of teaching goes on at this time of the day?" her mother was still angry.

Namukose looked at her mother in silence. Why was she being asked questions of this kind? "I came running all the way. Bogere isn't even here yet, but no one seems worried about him," she responded.

"This is about you, not Bogere, so leave him out of it," scolded Mrs Mukose.

"What is the difference between him and me?" Namukose asked.

"The difference between him and you is that he is a boy and you are a girl. There are a lot of traps which girls have to avoid. You need to be very careful."

"Traps are for animals not people," said Namukose.

"Don't annoy me, Namukose," her mother said, her voice rising.

But Mrs Mukose understood that Namukose was a good girl. She felt that she should not be too hard on her, so she let her anger go and said, speaking in a softer tone, "My daughter, I always get worried whenever you come home late. Mothers are responsible for whatever happens to their daughters. Anything can happen to you. When I was your age, I remember a friend of mine who got pregnant. She was not married. Her father was very annoyed. As a result, he beat her and her mother."

"What had the mother done?" Namukose asked.

"He claimed that the mother knew what her daughter had been doing behind his back."

Namukose looked at her mother with eyes wide open in surprise. "This is unbelievable," she said. "What does that have to do with the mother? Why should mothers suffer on behalf of their children?"

"You are also the first-born child. There is a belief that if the first-born girl in a family conceives outside marriage then the rest of the girls follow suit."

"That is not true," Namukose disagreed.

"Do you see why I want you home early?"

"I understand Mama."

"You can go and eat your food now."

Namukose went to eat with her heart heavy. She did not like to upset her mother, but she had so much work to do. Primary Seven was not easy. "I guess I will have to try my best to get home on time," she thought to herself.

But that was easier said than done. The very next day at school she found it difficult to concentrate on her work. She kept thinking of her mother and the girl who was beaten for becoming pregnant. She wondered whether any one beat the boy who made her pregnant. Life was difficult for girls, she thought. She was thinking of all these things when bell rang. The moment she heard it she knew what it meant.

"Pay attention to your work, Namukose!" snapped the teacher. "I know you are only thinking of going home now. Let me assure you, however, that you are not going home unless you finish your work."

What am I going to tell my mother? Namukose wondered.

In spite of all the challenges that came her way, Namukose always pushed on with her studies, no matter what obstacles she faced. When her courage started to dip, she would talk to her mother. Even when her mother did not encourage her in words, sometimes, just seeing her mother work hard, and remembering the Women's Day speech from Dr Kalembe, Namukose found the strength to continue working. She knew she had no option but to pass and pass highly so that she could get into a good secondary school – preferably a boarding school, where she would have time to concentrate on her studies.

At night, she revised for long hours by the light of a kerosene lamp. Sometimes she would be so tired that she would doze off. One day she almost burnt her hair that way!

At school, the pupils were given many tests to prepare them for the final exam. They had a test every month at first. As the exams drew nearer, these turned into weekly tests. Practice makes perfect, so they had to practice examinations until they were perfect.

As if all the reading she had to do was not enough for poor Namukose, there were a lot of other challenges as well. Her mother understood and even told her she was relieved of some of her chores. But Namukose would not allow it. She knew there was a lot of work to be done around the house, and her mother was not able to do it alone. There was no one to help her. Not her father, who spent all day in town and only came home to complain when the work was not done. And certainly not Bogere, who spent all his time playing. He never felt the pressure to study, and when Namukose had asked him if he would help his mother with chores, he laughed as if she had told him a hilarious joke.

Relief came in the form of a visit.

Namaganda, Namukose's friend who had been married off to a rich man just a couple of months before came to visit Namukose one day and found her friend looking tired and weary.

Namukose tried to be cheerful and asked, "How is married life, Namaganda?"

And her friend replied in the same way, trying to be cheerful and optimistic, she said it was fine. She was trying to get used to it. But it was not easy forgetting the opportunities that she missed. Namaganda felt miserable every time she thought about school, and about all the dreams her and Namukose used to dream as they walked home from school together. She said to her friend, "Namukose, it is up to you now. You are the one to make these dreams come true. For both of us. You must succeed, both for yourself and for me."

Namukose sighed. "I am trying my best. But it is hard. There is so much work to do but there is no time. I have home to worry about as well. I need to revise and to do my homework and study for weekly tests, but there is also work here at home. Somebody needs to help mother," she said. She sounded so sad, thought Namaganda. And she looked so tired.

That is when Namaganda made up her mind. She moved closer to her friend and put her hand over her shoulder. "Do not worry about your chores at home. You focus on your studies," she said, firmly. "If you promise to pass your exams for me, I will also do something for you."

From that day on, Namaganda would come to the Mukose's house every morning to help Mrs Mukose, just so that Namukose would have enough time to study.

Namukose was moved by her friend's generosity, but even more than that, she was inspired to continue working. Because now she knew that she was not only doing it for herself, she was doing it for all the girls in her area who never got the opportunity to get a full education.

Finally the big day – or rather the big two days of the exams – came. The rest of the school was closed and all the pupils who were not in Primary Seven were told to stay at home so that the candidates would be able to work in peace.

The night before that, Namukose went to bed early on a full stomach. Her mother and her friend Namaganda had prepared a special meal for her. Her father also came home early and sat next to her in the yard. He did not talk much but he put his hand on her shoulder and told her, in a quiet voice, "Namukose, good luck."

Just those three words meant more than a thousand books to Namukose.

She took those words with her to the exam room, along with the prayers of her beloved mother and her friends, and all the hard work she had put in, not only in the run up to the exams, but all the way from Primary One. She carried them with her as she walked to school the morning of her first paper.

The exams were being held in the new classroom buildings which had been built for the school by the Sheffield Church of Saint Stephen. They had been swept and mopped and given an extra-careful clean by the other students of the school. The room gleamed in the morning sunlight. Yes, even the sun shone bright for the candidates that day. It was as if even God himself wanted to reassure the candidates that there was nothing to worry about and that he wished them the best.

Of course Namukose and her fellow pupils were nervous, but all of this helped them relax a bit more. At least Namukose could think of her mother and remember why she must not fail.

Each candidate had a special desk all to himself or herself. It was not like the days when they were crowded five to a desk. There was plenty of space this time. In fact each desk was placed a good distance from the next one. This was done to prevent copying.

Each desk had the pupil's name written on it. Namukose sat at the desk with the words 'Namukose Lucy' and her index number and smiled to herself. Her nervousness was ebbing, because she was now feeling confident.

The first paper was English. The invigilator asked all the pupils to sit down and make sure they did not have any pieces of paper or books around them. The only thing they were allowed to have was a pen.

The invigilator brought in a large envelope. The pupils gasped silently in their hearts because they knew that inside the envelope were their examinations.

The invigilator was a serious man who did not smile when he brought the envelope in and placed it on the teacher's desk. He had to open it in front of everyone so that they could see that it had not been opened before.

He then took the papers out and distributed them to each pupil, one at a time. When he finally reached Namukose's desk, she realised that she had been holding her breath.

The papers were placed face downwards on the desk until every pupil had got his or hers. When every student had a paper, the invigilator announced to the classroom:

"You may now begin!"

Namukose turned the paper over and looked at the first question. She could not believe it. After seven years, the exams were finally starting....

She put her pen to the exam paper and began.

The exams ended the next day. The pupils were overjoyed and when the invigilator finally allowed them out of the exam room. They ran out and screamed with joy. They leapt up and down and hugged one another shouting, "We have finished! We have finished!" They were happy that their hard work of the candidate year was through, but they were also excited that they had finally finished primary school once and for all! Namukose ran and jumped along with all her friends. They had made it!

Chapter Seven

There was a long holiday now that school was over. Even though Namukose didn't think of it as school being over. She was confident that that she would be attending secondary school in a few months time.

She spent her time helping her mother at home. She also helped her brother Bogere with his schoolwork. She was glad to see that he was beginning to take it more seriously. She remembered how lazy he used to be – always playing – but now he wanted to be like his elder sister, after he saw how everybody had encouraged her.

Namukose also took the time to weave more mats to sell. She would keep the money she made from the mats in a safe place. She was going to use it when the time came to go to secondary school.

Finally, at the end of the year, the results for Primary Leaving Examinations came out. Namukose was eager to find out how she had performed. She woke up very early to get ready to go to her school, where the results were being displayed.

She left the home and began the familiar walk to school, smiling as she remembered all the days she walked this road in school uniform. She was quite lost in her own thoughts, dreaming of a wonderful secondary school, when she bumped into her friend Namaganda.

Namukose had not seen Namaganda for a very long time. Not since exams. She had just stopped coming to visit. Namukose's mother had said that Namaganda was a wife now and could not spend all her time visiting. She had a household and a husband to look after. Namukose was not too young to understand what that meant – that meant that Namaganda's husband did not allow her to visit.

So this was the first time in many months that Namukose was seeing her old friend. She smiled and hugged her and the greeted each other with joyful words, but there was a tinge of sadness there. Namaganda had got married to a man almost her father's age. She was the second wife. Life was hard for her. She was poorly dressed and looked much older than she actually was. She kept arching her back, and Namukose could see why. She was a few months pregnant and it showed through her tattered dress.

"You are lucky to still be in school," Namaganda said. "Life is not easy for some of us at all. My in-laws expect me to work like a donkey. I have to fetch water for myself and my in-laws. Every day I am reminded of the bride price they paid to my parents."

"That is funny," said Namukose.

"It is not funny at all," Namaganda objected. "It is tough. If only there was a way I would go back to school. But money is a big problem in the home."

"I thought you married a rich man," Namukose said.

Namaganda shook her head. "Well, he doesn't share his wealth with us his wives."

"Why don't you rear chickens like we were taught at school?" suggested Namukose.

"My husband slaughters one whenever he feels like."

"You mean you eat chicken all the time?"

"Women are not supposed to eat chicken," Namaganda said.

"Why?" Namukose asked.

"My husband says it makes them greedy. He says that everything in his house is his property, me inclusive, because he paid bride price."

Namukose laughed a dry laugh.

"Are you amused?" Namaganda asked. "I consider what he says to be an insult."

"I know," Namukose agreed.

"He complains that I am proud."

"Why does he think that you are proud?"

"He says it is because I went to school up to Primary Six whereas he stopped only in Primary Three. He says that he would dehorn me and put me in my right place."

"Which one is that?"

"I do not even bother to ask."

"Why don't you go back to your parents' home?"

"My mother says that is how all women are treated! That you just have to learn to be resilient."

"How about your father?"

"There is no way he would be able to pay back the bride price in case I left. And my brother is even worse. When I complained about my husband, he wanted to beat me instead," she said. Tears were beginning to well up in her eyes.

"Who can help you then?" Namukose asked.

"I do not know. I am completely helpless." She put her hand on her belly and looked softly at it and the baby growing within her. "Do you remember what the senior woman teacher used to tell us?" asked Namaganda. "She used to say that life was not that easy, especially for girls. Now I see what she meant. My in-laws want their son to marry another wife."

"Why?"

"He needs more help on the farm."

"Why not hire people to help instead?"

"There is no money to waste. A wife provides free labour."

"My dear, you have a lot to put up with."

"Yes, my friend. I have to run along now, otherwise my husband will beat me for staying too long on the way," Namaganda said.

As they parted, Namukose's heart was heavy. She felt so sad that her friend, who had started school before her, was now stuck in that life. She remembered how it was Namaganda who made her want to go to school when she showed her how to write her name. As she continued to school, her steps were heavy.

When she got to the school, there was a lot of excitement in the air. The pupils were dancing around. When the teachers saw her they had broad smiles on

58

their faces. Miss Nandase cheered loudly and beckoned her over. "My daughter, my daughter, come and give me a hug! Congratulations!" She wrapped Namukose in a warm embrace!

"You got a first grade, my daughter! You got the best mark in the whole school! My daughter, I am so proud of you! You have made us all proud!"

Namukose was overjoyed and tears washed down her face. The teachers and those of her classmates who were there were dancing around. Mr Bateganya stood in front of the schoolhouse smiling. He was very pleased. This was the first UPE class to sit for PLE and those who passed had succeeded against great odds.

They danced and laughed and talked about all the years they had gone through together. Those who had not done very well were encouraged by those who passed.

When Namukose went back home with the good news both her parents were happy, and so was Bogere. Her neighbours came over to congragulate her.

There was a lot of joy in the home on that day, but there was more joy to come in the life of young Lucy Namukose, the hardworking young girl who dedicated herself to her education and made sure she never gave up no matter how hard things became. In spite of all the obstacles of poverty and the obstacles caused by being a girl in a world where girls were considered second-rate, or treated like mere property, Lucy was determined to succeed. And just as she succeeded through her primary school, she beat the odds throughout secondary school. She won a scholarship thanks to her mentor Dr Robinah Kalembe, and had her fees paid all the way to university, where she became the first person of either gender from the village of Buwabe to graduate from university. She became Dr Lucy Namukose, and was able to use her education to earn enough money so that, together with Bogere, who was inspired by his sister to work hard too they managed to buy land and build a house for their father and mother. And it was when she was invited as guest of honour at Women's Day celebrations in the area that she announced that she was standing for Member of Parliament for the region. Dr Lucy Namukose had triumphed over the odds.